The Story of the Giant's Causeway

This story was adapted by author Ann Carroll
and illustrated by Derry Dillon

IRELAND'S BEST KNOWN STORIES

IN A
NUTSHELL

Published 2013
by: In a Nutshell
an imprint of Poolbeg Press Ltd

123 Grange Hill, Baldoyle
Dublin 13, Ireland

Text © Poolbeg Press Ltd 2013

1

A catalogue record for this book is available from the British Library.

ISBN 978 1 84223 599 7

Cover design and illustrations by Derry Dillon
Printed by GPS Colour Graphics Ltd, Alexander Road, Belfast BT6 9HP

This book belongs to

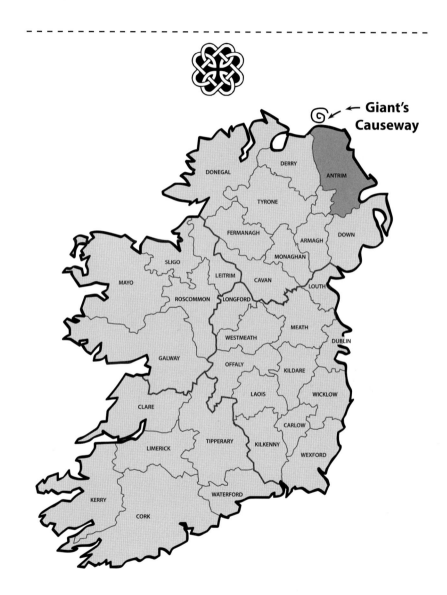

Giant's Causeway

DONEGAL
DERRY
ANTRIM
TYRONE
FERMANAGH
ARMAGH
DOWN
MONAGHAN
SLIGO
LEITRIM
CAVAN
LOUTH
MAYO
ROSCOMMON
LONGFORD
MEATH
WESTMEATH
DUBLIN
GALWAY
OFFALY
KILDARE
LAOIS
WICKLOW
CLARE
CARLOW
LIMERICK
TIPPERARY
KILKENNY
WEXFORD
KERRY
WATERFORD
CORK

Also in the Nutshell series

In the far north of Ireland, at the edge of the sea in Antrim, stands the Giant's Causeway. Raised above the level of the water and formed by forty thousand stone pillars, it is an extraordinary sight! The tallest of the columns is forty metres high. Most are six-sided, but others have four to eight sides and all are flat-topped. When visitors arrive they cannot resist walking on this unique road.

All the old stories say the causeway was the work of Fionn Mac Cumhaill, who was leader of the band of warriors called the Fianna. Fionn was famous for his strength and bravery. It seems he was also gigantic! His stone boot, left on one of the pillars, shows he was at least twenty-seven metres tall. But, most of all, Fionn was famous for his wisdom, for he had tasted the Salmon of Knowledge and knew everything! Well, almost everything. For when it came to love he was quite foolish.

Fionn was living on the coast of Antrim and was married to a perfectly fine, reliable woman called Oonagh. It's thought she was a lot smaller than him for he looked down on her a bit and used to daydream of meeting a lady who could look him straight in the eye.

Then one bright and sunny day, as he was staring out to sea, he saw on the cliffs of Scaffa, an island off Scotland, a beautiful lady giant. She took his breath away with her width, her height, her flashing eyes.

Fionn waved at her and she waved back. Encouraged, he waved twice as vigorously and jumped up and down. The lady giant did the same.

At this, Fionn lost the head entirely and roared across the water, "Come here to me at once!"

Well, the lady giant wasn't a bit keen on swimming over and getting herself soaked through and she indicated as much.

"Don't worry! I'll fix everything!" Fionn yelled and he lifted huge stones and flung them into the water to make a causeway so his new beloved wouldn't get her huge feet wet.

But before it was finished he saw to his dismay that the lady giant had disappeared. For while she wasn't against waving across the sea and jumping up and down in a friendly manner, she was none too keen on having huge stones hurled in her direction by a strange gigantic man. And anyway she had her own husband-giant at home.

That's one story about how Fionn made the Giant's Causeway, but there is another story, one that's more popular with people who love tales about fighting and smart planning and wives who are worth their weight in gold.

One day as Fionn was staring across the sea, looking for something to do, he saw on the coast of Scotland an extremely ugly giant who was broader and taller and bigger all round than he was himself.

"I like a challenge," Fionn mused, "and life is very boring at the minute, with none of the Fianna here and Oonagh wanting me to do domestic things like turning the house right round to face the sea." He took another look at the Scottish giant. "I've never seen anyone as ugly! How many eyebrows does the fellow have? His arms are like huge trees. I'd say he'd be a good fighter though!"

With that Fionn began hurling insults across the sea. "Hey, you! Tiny! Bristle-brows! Coward!"

The Scottish giant was raging. "Get my name right!" he roared. "I'm Benandonner, the biggest giant on the face of the earth! No one calls me Tiny and gets away with it! If I could swim I'd be over there to pulverise you!"

"Don't let a drop of water stop you!" Fionn yelled back, delighted at the prospect of a proper fight. "I'll make a bridge you can cross."

With that, he lifted a great clump of earth and hurled it towards Scotland. It dropped miles short and was later known as the Isle of Man. The hole it left in the ground filled with water and is called Lough Neagh to this day.

Fionn then lifted huge pillar-like stones and flung them over one by one until they formed a causeway Benandonner could cross. But at this stage he was feeling very tired, while the Scottish giant was fresh and still raging.

Benandonner strode across, ready to demolish his enemy. The closer he got the more enormous he seemed. Fionn's wisdom got the better of his desire for battle.

I'm exhausted, he thought, and in no fit state to fight. He'll destroy me.

So he turned on his heel and made for home where he explained the situation to Oonagh.

"Right!" his fine, reliable wife said as she draped a white cloth over the very large bathtub. "Get in here."

"Why?"

"Because I'm going to disguise you as a baby and this is the crib."

Now, Fionn trusted his wife and since he could hear Benandonner's large feet pounding towards the house he put up no argument.

Oonagh tucked him into the bathtub with a blanket, put a bonnet on his head and tied the ribbon under his chin.

He makes a dreadful-looking baby, she thought. Truly shocking! But she hoped for the best.

"Best pretend to be asleep," she said.

Just then the door burst open and Benandonner had to stoop to squeeze himself into the house.

"Where's that fellow who was so free with his insults?" he roared.

"Shhhh! Hush at once! You'll wake the baby. Is it Fionn Mac Cumhaill you mean? He's gone off hunting."

"Well, I'll wait." Benandonner tried to whisper but it was like the rumble of a threatening volcano. He stared at the bathtub. "That's a huge baby! I've never seen the like."

"Fionn's child," Oonagh said proudly.
"Takes after his father for strength. Do you
know, if there was a Strong Baby competition,
this one would win it!"

Benandonner looked less sure of himself. After all, if this was the child, the father must be colossal altogether! From the coast of Scotland he hadn't looked huge. The distance must have made him look much smaller! Maybe a fight wasn't such a good idea. Losing would be very painful.

But just as he was thinking of going, Oonagh said, "You're a fine massive fellow. I bet you can do really strong things."

"I can!" Benandonner puffed with pride. "Give me any test of strength and I'll pass it."

Oonagh pretended to think. At last she said, "I bet you couldn't lift up this house and turn it around so that the front is facing the sea!"

"I bet I could!" said Benandonner.

He went outside and wrapped his arms around the large stone house. He puffed with exertion as he heaved the building up from the ground and staggered about in a circle till it was properly facing the sea.

"Well done!" said Oonagh. "Come inside and have a bite to eat. You must be tired out!"

"Not at all!" said the giant, but his legs were very wobbly and he staggered into the house.

Oonagh prepared a large steak, but while he wasn't looking she painted a big flat stone to look like a magnificent piece of meat.

At this stage Benandonner was nearly nodding off with tiredness and without much examination he bit into what he thought was fine beef.

"Aaaagh!" Two of his huge front teeth broke and he was fully awake again.

"What's the matter?" Oonagh said as she tossed the real steak over to the so-called baby, who ate it in three bites.

Benandonner was astounded. If that infant can eat something that breaks my teeth, he thought, his father must be very strong altogether!

And I don't think I want to meet him. So he turned to Oonagh and said, "I have to go now. They'll be looking for me at home."

"It was lovely having you visit," Oonagh told him. "It's a pity you missed Fionn. You must come again when he's here. But at least say goodbye to the baby before you go."

Benandonner wasn't much good with babies but he was very keen to leave and knew he'd never get away from a mother without admiring her child first.

"A fine baby," he said without much sincerity. In fact he thought it was a brute of a baby. "It's great he could gobble that steak!"

"Ah, that's because he has a few small teeth. Put your finger into his mouth – gently now – and you'll feel them at the edge of his gums."

Benandonner did so, curious. With a sudden snap of his jaw the 'baby' bit off his finger.

Howling with pain, Benandonner pushed through the door without a word of goodbye, rushed down to the sea and ran all the way across the causeway, tearing up most of the

stones behind him with his good hand, so he wouldn't be followed by the terrible infant's more terrible father. And what he left of the causeway remains to this day.

Geologists believe it all happened differently. They say that sixty-five million years ago a volcano erupted. A flow of lava rose through a chalky bed, then met the icy water. As the lava cooled, it cracked and snapped to form all the columns that are the Giant's Causeway.

Science or legend – which is closest to the truth? Maybe the stories are. After all, Fionn's boot is still there, a witness to the past.

The End

Word Sounds in The Giant's Causeway

Words	Sounds
Fionn:	Fee-un
Mac:	Mock
Cumhaill:	Cool
Scaffa:	Sca-fa
Benandonner:	Ben – an – don – er
Oonagh:	Oo – na. Una

Also available from the **IN A NUTSHELL** series

All you need to know about Ireland's best loved stories in a nutshell

Available Now!

Available Now!

Available Now!

Available Now!

Available Now!